THE
TRIAL

Of the Notorious Highwayman

Richard Turpir

At *York* Aſſizes, on the 22d Day ᴏ
March, 1739, before the Hon. Sir WILLIAᴎ
CHAPPLE, Kt. Judge of Aſſize, and one ᴄ
His Majeſty's Juſtices of the Court of King
Bench.

Taken down in Court by Mr. THOMAS KYLL
Profeſſor of Short Hand.

To which is prefix'd,

An exact Account of the ſaid *Turpin*, from hⁱ
firſt coming into *Yorkſhire*, to the Time of hⁱ
being committed Priſoner to *York* Caſtle; com
municated by Mr. APPLETON of *Beverleʸ*
Clerk of the Peace for the *Eaſt-Riding* of tⁱ
ſaid County.

With a Copy of a Letter which *Turpin* receiνe
from his Father, while under Sentence of Deat

To which is added,

His Behaviour at the Place of Execution, on *Saturday* the 7
of *April*, 1739. Together with the whole Confeſſion
made to the Hangman at the Gallows; wherein he ;
knowledg'd himſelf guilty of the Facts for which he ſuffer
own'd the Murder of Mr. *Thompſon*'s Servant on *Eppiⁱ*
Foreſt, and gave a particular Account of ſeveral Robbe
which he had committed.

The following Account of Turpin *wa*
communicated to the Publishers by M
Robert Appleton, *of* Beverley, *Cler.*
of the Peace for the East-Riding *o*
the County of York ; *to whose inde*
fatigable Care and Diligence the Pub
lick are very much oblig'd, for thi
notorious Offender's being brought ı
Justice.

'**A**BOUT two Years ago, a Person can
'   out of *Lincolnshire* to *Brough*, ne
'   *Market-Cave* in *Yorkshire*, and sta
' for some Time at the Ferry-House in *Broug*
' and said his Name was *John Palmer* ; and
' went from thence sometimes to live at *Nort.*
' *Cave*, and sometimes at *Welton* ; and cont
' nued at these Places about fifteen or sixte
' Months, except such Part of the Time as
' went into *Lincolnshire* to see his Friends, as
' pretended, which in that Time he very oft
' did, and frequently brought three or four H(
' ses back with him, which he used to sell
' exchange in *Yorkshire* ; and while he so liv
' at *Brough*, *Cave*, and *Welton*, he very of
' went out a Hunting and Shooting with sev
' Gentlemen in the Neighbourhood ; and in
' Beginning of *October* last, as he was returr
' from Shooting, he saw one of his Landlo
' Cocks in the Town-Street, which he shot

and killed; and one *Hall*, his Neighbour, seeing him shoot the Cock, said to him, *Mr. Palmer, you have done wrong in shooting your Landlord's Cock:* Whereupon *Palmer* said to him, *If he would only stay whilst he had charged his Piece, he would shoot him too.* Mr. *Hall* hearing him say so, went and told the Landlord what *Palmer* had done and said; thereupon the Landlord immediately went with the said *Hall* to Mr. *Crowle*, and got his Warrant for apprehending the said *Palmer*, by Virtue of which Warrant he was next Day taken up and carried to the General Quarter Sessions, then holden at *Beverley*, where he was examined by *George Crowle, Hugh Bethel*, and *Marmaduke Constable*, Esqrs. three of his Majesty's Justices of the Peace for the *East-Riding of Yorkshire*, and they demanding Sureties for his good Behaviour, and he refusing to find Sureties, was by them then committed to the House of Correction; which Commitment was in the Words following, *To the Master, or Keeper, of the House of Correction in* Beverley; *Whereas it appears to us, upon the Informations of divers credible Persons, That* John Palmer, *of* Welton, *in the* East-Riding *of the County of* York, *is a very dangerous Person, and we having required Sureties for his good Behaviour until the next General Quarter Sessions of the Peace to be held for the* East-*Riding of the County of* York, *which he the said* John Palmer *hath refused to find; These are therefore to command you, to receive into your Custody the Body of the said* John Pal-

mer, *and him safely keep, until he shall be di*
charged by due Course of Law ; and here
fail not at your Peril. Given under on
Hands and Seals the third Day of October
1738. The Gentlemen having taken sever:
Informations from Persons of *Brough* and *We*
ton, about *Palmer*'s frequently going into *Li*
colnshire, and usually returning with Plenty (
Money, and several Horses, which he sold (
exchanged in *Yorkshire,* had just Reason to fu
spect, that he was either a Highwayman (
Horse-Stealer ; and being desirous to do the
Country Justice, and fearful to oppress the I
nocent, the next Day went to the said *Jol*
Palmer, and examined him again, touchin;
where he had lived, and to what Business h
was brought up ? Who then said, *He had abo*
two Years before lived at Long-Sutton *i*
Lincolnshire, *and was by Trade a Butcher*
That his Father then lived at Long-Sutton
and his Sister kept his Father's House there
but he having contracted a great many Debt
for Sheep that proved rotten, so that he w
not able to pay for them, he therefore w
obliged to abscond, and come and live in Yorl
shire. The Justices, upon this Confessic
thought it the properest Way to send a M
senger into *Lincolnshire,* to enquire into tl
Truth of this Matter ; and Mr. *Rob*
Appleton, Clerk of the Peace for the f
Riding, then wrote a Letter to *Long-Sutt*
signifying the whole Affair ; which Letter v
sent by a special Messenger, and given to (
Mr. *Delamere,* a Justice of the Peace, who

ved there; and Mr. *Appleton* received a Letter from him in Anſwer thereto, with this Account, *That the ſaid* John Palmer *had lived there about three Quarters of a Year, and was accuſed before him of Sheep-ſtealing, whereupon he iſſued out his Warrant againſt* Palmer; *who was thereupon apprehended, but made his Eſcape from the Conſtable; and ſoon after ſuch his Eſcape, Mr.* Delamere *had ſeveral Informations lodged before him againſt the ſaid* Palmer, *for Suſpicion of Horſe-ſtealing: And that* Palmer's *Father did not live at* Long-Sutton, *neither did he know where he lived, therefore deſired* Palmer *might be ſecured, and he would make further Inquiry about the Horſes ſo ſtolen, and he would bind over ſome Perſons to proſecute him at the next Aſſizes.* Upon the Receipt of Mr. *Delamere's* Letter, Mr. *Appleton* immediately ſent a Meſſenger to Mr. *Crowle*, who came to *Beverley* next Morning, and finding *Palmer* to be ſo great a Villain, did not think it ſafe for him to ſtay any longer in *Beverley* Houſe of Correction, ſo Mr. *Appleton* required him again to find Sureties for his Appearance at the next Aſſizes; and for Want thereof, he made his Commitment to *York* Caſtle, which Mr. *Crowle* and Captain *Appleyard* then ſign'd, and he was that Morning, *viz.* 16th *October*, 1738, ſent away from the Houſe of Correction to *York* Caſtle, Handcuffed, and under the Guard of *George Smith* and *Joſhua Milner*, who were directed by Mr. *Appleton* to conduct him ſafe to *York* Caſtle, and did it accordingly. About

a Month after *Palmer* was sent from *Beverle*
House of Correction to *York* Castle, Two Per
sons came out of *Lincolnshire*, and challenge
a Mare and Foal which *Palmer* had sold t
Captain *Dawson* of *Ferraby*, and also th
Horse which *Palmer* rode on when he cam
to *Beverley*, to be stolen from them off *Hick*
ington Fenn in *Lincolnshire*. And, about fou
Months after he was committed to *York* Castle
he was discovered to be *TURPIN*, the No
torious Highwayman, by a Letter being i:
tercepted, which he had wrote to his Sist
in *Essex*.

Erratum in the **TRIAL.**

Page 6. *Line* 8. *Read thus* ; Yes, it was
Black-Ball.

OPY of a Letter from *John Turpin*
to his Son *Richard Turpin*, Prifoner
in *York* Caftle.

March 29. 1739.

Dear Child,

Received your Letter this Inftant, with
a great deal of Grief; according to
ur Requeft, I have writ to your Brother
hn, and Madam Peck, to make what
terceffion can be made to Col. Watfon,
order to obtain Tranfportation for
ur Misfortune; which had I 100 l.
would freely part with it to do you
ood; in the mean Time my Prayers for
u, and for God's Sake, give your whole
ind to beg of God to pardon your many
ranfgreffions, which the Thief upon the
ofs received Pardon for at the laft Hour,
o' a very great Offender. The Lord be
ur Comfort, and receive you into his
rnal Kingdom.

I am your Diftrefs'd,
Yet Loving Father,
JOHN TURPIN.

lemftead,

THE

TRIAL

OF

John Palmer, alias *Paumer,* alias *Richard Turpin,*

At the Assizes holden at the Castle of York, in and for the said County, the 22d Day of March, 1738-9, before the Hon. Sir WILLIAM CHAPPLE, *Kt. Judge of Assize, and One of His Majesty's Justices of the Court of King's Bench.*

The JURY.

William Calvert,	*Thomas Simpson,*
Samuel Waddington,	*George Smeaton,*
William Popplewell,	*Robert Thompson,*
John Lambert,	*William Frank,*
Robert Wiggin,	*James Boyes,*
William Wade,	*Thomas Clarke.*

JOhn Palmer, alias *Paumer,* alias *Richard Turpin,* was indicted for stealing a Black Mare and Foal, at *Welton,* in the County

The Counsel for the King, THOMAS PLA⟨
Esq; Recorder of the City of *York*, and Ric⟨
ARD CROWLE, of the *Inner-Temple*, Esq; ha⟨
ing open'd the Nature of the Indictment, p⟨
ceeded to the Examination of Witnesses, as f⟨
lows, *viz.*

Thomas Creasey (the Owner of the Mare.)⟨

Counsel. Where do you live?

Creasey. At *Heckington*, in the County ⟨
Lincoln.

Coun. Pray, Sir, had you a Mare and a Foa⟨
Crea. Yes.

Coun. Where did they go or feed?

Crea. Upon *Heckington* Common.

Coun. When did you first miss them?

Crea. Upon a *Thursday* Morning I was enqu⟨
ing for them, and they could not be found.

Coun. What Day of the Month do you thi⟨
it might happen?

Crea. Upon the 18th or 19th Day of *Augu⟨*
Coun. What Month?

Crea. The Month of *August* last.

Coun. You say you missed them on *Thursd⟨*
the 18th or 19th of *August* last; pray then, S⟨
when did you see them last?

Crea. The Day next before I lost them.

Coun. When you then missed your Mare a⟨
Foal, what did you do in order to get Intel⟨
gence about them?

Crea. I hired Men and Horses, and rode for⟨
Miles round about us, to hear of them, and g⟨
them cry'd in all the Market Towns about us.

Crea. One *John Baxter*, a Neighbour of mine, told me, he had been at *Pocklington* Fair in *Yorkshire*, and lying all Night at *Brough*, he happened to hear of a Man that was taken up and sent to the House of Correction at *Beverley*, for shooting a Game-Cock, who had such a Mare and Foal as mine: Upon which Information I came to *Ferraby*, near *Beverley*, and put up my Horse at *Richard Grafsby*'s, who keeps a publick House; and began to enquire of him about my Mare and Foal? Who told me, there was such a like Mare and Foal in their Neighbourhood; which I thought, by the Description he gave me, to be mine; so then I told him, I was come to enquire about such a Mare and Foal.

Coun. Did you know the Marks of the Mare and Foal, as he described them to you?

Crea. Yes, I did; and told him these Marks agreed with my Mare and Foal, before I did see them.

Coun. Was it when your Neighbour came home, you made this Inquiry?

Crea. Yes, it was; and by this Information of his, I went to *Ferraby*, and gave the Landlord and People an Account of their Marks.

Court. Describe their Marks.

Crea. She was a Black Mare, blind of the near Eye, having a little White on the near Fore-Foot, and also the near Hind Foot, a little above the Hoof, and scratch'd, (*greased*) on both the Hind Feet, and the near Fore-Foot, with I's, or Marks resembling that Letter, burnt on the near Shoulder, and a Star on the Forehead.

Coun. How long have you had her?

Crea. I did breed her myself, and kept l 'till she was ten Years old.

Court. Did you give this Account to *Richa Grafsby,* before he shewed you her?

Crea. Yes, I did.

Court. Had the Foal any Marks?

Crea. Yes, it was black-ball.

Coun. Where did you see her?

Crea. At the Stable Door they fetcht her o to me, and I knew her.

Court. From all these Marks are you very p sitive the Mare and Foal was yours?

Crea. Yes, I am sure they were mine.

Court. Did you receive them at that Time

Crea. No, I did not get them then.

Court. Are you sure the Mare and Foal we yours?

Crea. Yes, indeed I am.

Court. When you came to *Ferraby,* did yc tell these Marks, or the Description of ther and to whom?

Crea. Yes, indeed, I told them to *Richar Grafsby* the Landlord.

Court to the Prisoner. Have you any Que tions to ask this Witness? You have heard wha ie has said against you.

Prisoner. I cannot say any Thing, for I hav iot any Witnesses come this Day, as I expecte herefore beg your Lordship to put off my Tri till another Day.

Court. We cannot now put off this Affair; ou had spoke, and desired a reasonable Tim efore the Jury was sworn and charged, it migh

ve been granted you —— Now you are too
hte, the Jury cannot be difcharged —— You
ive Liberty allowed you to ask any Queftions
i the Witnefs.

Prif. This Witnefs is wrong, becaufe on the
8th of *Auguft* I was here in *Tork* Caftle.

Coun. No, Sir, you was not here the 18th of
Auguft.

Mr. Griffith *the Goaler being call'd, inform'd
the Court, that it was* October *before* Palmer
was committed Prifoner to the Caftle.

Prif. I never did fee this Man *(Thomas
Creafey)* in my Life.

Prifoner to Creafey. Do you know one *Whitehead ?*

Crea. Yes.

Prif. He's the Man I bought the Mare and
Foal of.

Captain Dawfon *call'd,* —— 2d Witnefs.

Court. Pray, Sir, inform us what you know
f this Affair ?

Daw. I was one Morning riding to *Welton*
nd met a Man leading a Mare and Foal ; I ask'd
im, if that was his Mare and Foal? He told
he, No; but they belonged to one *Palmer*
asked him, if he would difpofe of the Foal
He faid, *Palmer* was coming up the Street ——
turned about, and faw *Palmer* ; who told me
was his Mare and Foal, and they were bred in
Lincolnfhire. I asked, if he would difpofe of th
Foal ? He faid, he would rather fell the Mare
ith her. I reply'd, I had no Occafion for th
Mare, only the Foal, and asked the Price of th

Foal? He said, Three Guineas. I told him, was too much to ask for the Foal, and offer him two Guineas, and said I would not give hi more; upon which I went about my Busine and afterwards I obferved the Prifoner coming u a Hill with the Mare and Foal; and, as I w going along, a Country Man faid, Sir, You ha been about bargaining, and bid two Guineas f the Foal; you'll fee him come back again, an if you pleafe, I fancy you may have it. I fai Let him come to my Houfe, and I will pay hi the two Guineas: So about Three o' Clock the Afternoon, he came with the Mare an Foal, and I had them both put in a Stable; went then to pay the Prifoner *Palmer*.

Coun. Pray who was it that brought the Ma and Foal to your Houfe?

Daw. Nobody brought the Mare and Foal t me but himfelf. I went, and paid him for th Foal two Guineas; and then he told me, night buy the Mare, for fhe was worth Money I told him, I had no Occafion for the Mare but the Prifoner being a little preffing about i told him I had a Horfe of no great Value, an f he would change, or let me have the Mare t urfe the Foal, I would rather do it. He di ot like the firft Propofal, but I told him, vould not take the Mare except he would hav he Horfe, fo I gave him four Guineas; but be ig obliged to go to my Regiment, I left th lace foon after.

Coun. When did you leave the Country?

Daw. Soon after, I think about *October* I wen

away

ay, and gave *Richard Grafsby* the Care of
e Mare, and he had the Liberty to work her.
Court. Have you any Thing to fay as to what
e Captain hath faid againft you?

Prif. Nothing at all.

Richard Grafsby, ———— 3d Witnefs.

Court. What have you to fay about the Mare

Graf. I had Liberty to work her.

Court. How long have you known the Pri:
oner?

Graf. I have feen him feveral Times fince, and
think, I have known him about two Years.

Coun. What Manner of vifible Living had he

Graf. He had no fettled Way of Living that :
now of at all; tho' a Dealer, yet he was :
ranger, and lived like a Gentleman.

Coun. Had you the Mare of Captain *Daw:*
on?

Graf. Yes, I had the Mare and Foal.

Coun. Did he give you Liberty to work her

Graf. Yes.

Coun. About what Time did you work her

Graf. About *October* the 12th, I think.

Coun. Did you work her?

Graf. Yes, I did, for I had a Clofe belongin
o the Captain.

Coun. Was the Mare challenged when yo
ad her?

Graf. Yes, fhe was; I had been drawir
with her, and *Thomas Creafey* came to me, ar
ave me an Account very fully of all her Mark

Coun. What! was you with him frequently?

Smith. Yes.

Coun. When did you fee him laft?

Smith. 'Tis about five Years fince I faw him.

Coun. Have you any particular Marks to fhew this is the Man?

Smith. This is the very Man.

Coun. Did you not teach him at School?

Smith. Yes, I did, but he was only learning to make Letters; and, I believe, he was three Quarters of a Year with me.

Coun. Do you think this is he?

Smith. Yes, this is the Man.

Coun. As you lived there, why did you come down here to this Place?

Smith. Happening to be at the Poft-Office where I faw a Letter directed to *Turpin's* Brother in Law, who, as I was informed, would not loofe the Letter and pay Poftage; upon that Account taking particular Notice thereof, I thought at firft I remembered the Superfcription, and concluded it to be the Hand-Writing of the Prifoner *Turpin*; whereupon I carried the Letter before a Magiftrate, who broke the fame open (the Letter was fubfcribed *John Palmer*) and found it fent from *York* Caftle: I had feen feveral of *Dick Turpin's* Bills, and knew his Hand.

Coun. Are you fure this is his Letter? (*A Letter produced in Court.*)

Smith. Yes, I am fure that is his Letter.

Coun. Was that the Caufe of your coming own?

Smith. Yes

Coun. How happen'd you to take Notice of this Letter?

Smith. Seeing the *York* Stamp.

Coun. From thefe Circumftances did you come down here?

Smith. Yes, indeed, I did come upon this Account.

Coun. When you came to the Caftle, did you challenge him, or know him?

Smith. Yes, I did, upon the firft View of him, and pointed him out from among all the reft of the Prifoners.

Coun. How long is it fince you faw him laft?

Smith. I think about five Years.

Coun. Do you know any Thing more of him?

Smith. I think he might be about eleven or twelve Years old, when I went to the Excife, and he worked with his Father, who was a Butcher.

Coun. Was he ever fet up in the Butcher Trade?

Smith. Yes, I know he was.

Coun. How long might he live in that Way?

Smith. I cannot tell; he lived at ——— †
in *Effex*, and left it about fix Years, and after he kept a Publick Houfe.

Coun. Did you afterwards fee him?

Smith. Yes, I faw him afterwards fix Miles from thence.

Coun. What became of him then?

Smith

---

† There was fuch a Noife in the Court, that the Gentlema

Smith. I do not know more, only the laſt Time I ſaw him, I ſold him a Grey Mare about five Years ago, before my Brother died.

Coun. Do you know no more of him?

Smith. This I know of him, and I have been many Times in his Company, and frequently with him.

Court. *Palmer*, you are allowed the Liberty to ask Mr. *Smith* any Queſtion.

Priſ. I never knew him.

When Mr. Smith *came firſt to* York, *in Fe-bruary laſt, he was examined at the Caſtle, by ſeveral of his Majeſty's Juſtices of Peace for this County, and gave them the ſame Account as above.*

Mr. Edward Saward, *of* Hempſtead *in* Eſſex, *call'd.*

Coun. Do you know this *Richard Turpin?*

Saw. Yes — I do know him; he was born and brought up at the *Bell*; his Father kept a Publick Houſe.

Coun. How long have you known him?

Saw. I have known him theſe twenty two Years; I cannot ſay I know exceeding exact, but about twenty two Years, upon my Soul: [*Here the Council reprov'd* Saward, *and ſaid to him,* Friend, You have ſworn once already, you need not ſwear again.] *Saward.* I knew him ever ſince he was a Boy, and lived at the *Bell*.

Coun. How long did he live there?

Saw. I cannot exactly tell; he lived with his Father, and I was very great with him.

Coun. Did you know him after he set up for himself?

Saw. Yes, I knew him perfectly well then, and I have bought a great many good Joints of Meat of him, upon my Soul!

Upon this the Judge reprimanded him, and advised him not to speak so rashly, but to consider he was upon Oath, and that he should speak seriously.

Coun. Did you know him since he left *Hempstead?*

Saw. I was with him at his House at *Hempstead.*

Coun. Did you see him there?

Saw. I saw him frequently, I can't tell how often.

Coun. How many Years is it since he left *Hempstead?*

Saw. He came backwards and forwards.

Coun. How long is it since you saw him last?

Saw. About five or six Years ago.

Coun. And can you say this assuredly or firmly?

Saw. Yes, and I never saw him since.

Coun. Had he any settled Dwelling?

Saw. Not that I know of.

Court. Now look to the Prisoner; is this *Richard Turpin?*

Saw. Yes, yes, *Dick Turpin,* the Son of *John Turpin,* who keeps the *Bell* at *Hempstead.*

Turpin deny'd he knew this Edward Saward *but seem'd at last to own Mr.* Smith.

Counsel to Mr. Smith. Mr. *Smith,* when you spoke to him in the Castle, did you know him

Smith. Yes, I did, and he did confess he knew me; and said unto me two or three Times. I *us bung our Eyes in Drink* ; and I drank with him, which is this *Richard Turpin.*

Court to Turpin. There was a Mare and Foal loft, what Account can you give, how you came by that Mare and Foal ?

Prif. I was going up to *Lincolnfhire* to *John Whitehead* ; there was a Mare and Foal before his Door, and I was there drinking.

Coun. Does he keep a Houfe, and fell Ale ?

Prif. Yes.

Coun. What Place was it at ?

Prif. Within a Mile of *Heckington.* — The Man had been at a Fair, and bought a Mare and Foal, and he wanted to fell them again.

Coun. What Time was it ?

Prif. In *Auguft* : I asked the Price, and gave him feven Guineas for Mare and Colt ; he gave me back Half a Crown ; I ftaid all Night, and came away next Morning. — I went to all Markets, and wherever I went, I rode with them, without ever being challenged.

Court. Have you any Thing more to fay ?

Prif. I have fent a *Subpæna* for a Man and his Wife, they were prefent when I bought them.

Court. What is his Name ?

Prif. I cannot tell, therefore I defire fome longer Time that thefe Witneffes may be examined. I alfo fent a fpecial Meffenger with a Letter.

[*Mr.* Griffith *the Jaylor being call'd, faid,* The Meffenger is come back.]

Court. What fay you to that ?

Prifoner was filent.

Court. If you have any Witneffes, you fhould

have had them here before this Time; have you any Witnesses here prefent?

Prif. I have none at prefent, but to Morrow I will have them; I am fure no Man can fay ill of me in *Yorkfhire.*

Court. Have you any Witnesses here?

Prif. Yes, *William Thompfon*, Efq; alfo one *Whitehead*, and one Mr. *Gill.*

All thefe were call'd in Court, *but did not appear.*

Court. The Jury cannot ftay, and you fee there is none appearing for you.

Prif. I thought I fhould have been removed to *Effex*, for I did not expect to be Tried in this Country, ; therefore I could not prepare Witneffes to my Character.

After this the Hon. Sir William Chapple *gave his Charge to the Jury.*

Prifoner. The Reafons I had for changing my Name, were, that I having been long out of Trade, and run my felf into Debt, I changed my Name to my Mother's, which was *Palmer.*

Court. What was your Name before you came to *Lincolnfhire* ?

Prifoner. Turpin.

Court. Was it *Richard Turpin* ?

Prifoner. Yes.

Prifoner. I thought I fhould have been removed, and got my Trial in *Effex.*

Court. You have deceived yourfelf in thinking fo.

The JURY immediately, without going out of Court, brought in their Verdict, GUILTY.

John **Palmer,** alias *Pawmer,* alias *Richard Turpin,* was indicted a Second Time, for stealing a Black Gelding, the Property of *Thomas Creasey.*

Court. CALL *Thomas Creasey.*] *Sir,* Was you in Possession of a Gelding in *August* last?

Crea. Yes, I was.

Coun. About what Time did you miss it?

Crea. The 18th Day of *August* I missed this Gelding.

Coun. Where did you find him, and what Colour was he?

Crea. I found him at the *Blue Bell* in *Beverley.*

Coun. How came you to hear he was there?

Crea. Richard Grasby was the Person that told me it was my Gelding.

Coun. Did you describe this Gelding to him?

Crea. Yes, and then he told me it was the same.

Coun. Upon that what did you do?

Crea. I went to the Landlord of the House at *Beverley,* and described him to him.

Coun. Do you remember what Description you gave him of the Gelding?

Crea. Yes, the Description was a black Gelding, with a little Star on his Forehead.

Coun. What did he (*the Landlord*) do then?

Crea. I went with him, and he shewed me the Horse.

Coun. Are you fure the Gelding he fhewed you was yours?

Crea. Yes, I am.

Coun. But are you very fure that was your Gelding?

Crea. Yes, yes; indeed, I am.

Coun. Did you fhew him to any Perfon?

Crea. Yes, I did; I fhewed him to *Carey Gill*, the Conftable at *Welton*.

Court to *Carey Gill*, the Conftable. What do you know concerning the Prifoner?

Gill. He was taken up by me for fhooting a Cock, upon which I carried him to *Beverley* Seffions.

Coun. Which Way did you carry him; or, how did he go?

Gill. He rode upon his own Horfe, and I along with him.

Coun. What Month did this happen in?

Gill. At *Michaelmas* Seffions, which was *October* the fixth.

Coun. Do you know what Horfe he rod upon?

Gill. He rode upon a Horfe which he called his own.

Coun. Did you fee that Horfe?

Gill. Yes, It was that fame Horfe he came from *Welton* upon.

Court to *Thomas Creafey.* How did you get your Horfe again?

Crea. I got him from the Juftice, by his Order.

Coun. How many Miles was it from Hor

Crea. It was about fifty Miles from the Wa-
ter-Side to *Welton.*

Coun. Was that the fame Horfe you heard de-
fcribed?

Crea. Yes, it was.

Coun. What Marks had he?

Crea. He was a black Gelding, with a little
ftar on his Forehead, and carried a good Tail.

Court to *James Smith.* How long is it
fince you have known the Prifoner at the Bar?
Look at him again.

Smith. I have known him from his Infancy,
thefe twenty two Years; and he is the very
Richard Turpin which I have known at *Hemp-
ftead;* and the very Son of *John Turpin* in that
Town.

Court to the *Prifoner.* Have you any more
to fay?

Prif. I bought this Horfe of *Whitehead.*

The *JURY* brought in their *Verdict,* and
and him GUILTY.

When the Judge was going to pafs Sentence,
the Prifoner was ask'd what Reafons he had to
give why Sentence of Death fhould not be pro-
nunc'd againft him.

Prifoner. It is very hard upon me, my Lord,
becaufe I was not prepar'd for my Defence.

Court. Why was you not? You knew the
time of the Affizes as well as any Perfon here.

Prif. Several Perfons who came to fee me,
affured me, that I fhould be removed to

it needless to prepare Witnesses for my Defence here.

Court. Whoever told you so were highly to blame ; and as your Country have found you guilty of a Crime worthy of Death, it is my Office to pronounce Sentence against you.

THE Morning before *Turpin*'s Execution he gave 3 *l.* 10 *s.* amongst five Men, who were to follow the Cart as Mourners, with Hatbands and Gloves, and gave Gloves and Hatbands to several Persons more. He also left a Gold Ring and two Pair of Shoes and Clogs to a married Woman at *Brough*, that he was acquainted with, though he at the same Time acknowledg'd he had a Wife and Child of his own.

He was carried in a Cart to the Place of Execution, on *Saturday, April* 7th, 1739, with *John Stead*, condemn'd also for Horse-Stealing ; he behav'd <u>himself</u> with amazing Assurance, and bow'd to the Spectators as he pass'd : It was remarkable that as he mounted the Ladder, his Right Leg trembled, on which he stamp'd it down with an Air, and with undaunted Courage look'd round about him ; and after speaking near Half an Hour to the Topsman, threw himself off the Ladder, and expired in about five Minutes.

His Corpse was brought back from the Gallows about Three in the Afternoon, and lodged at the *Blue Boar* in *Castlegate,* 'till Ten the next Morning, when it was buried in a neat Coffin in St. *George*'s Church-Yard, without *Fisher gate* Postern, with this Inscription, *J. P.* 173

R. T. aged 28 *. The Grave was dug very deep, and the Perſons whom he appointed his Mourners, as above-mention'd, took all poſſible Care to ſecure the Body; notwithſtanding which, on *Tueſday* Morning, about three o' Clock, ſome Perſons were diſcover'd to be moving off the Body, which they had taken up; and the Mob having got Scent where it was carried to, and ſuſpecting it was to be anatomiz'd, went to a Garden in which it was depoſited, and brought away the Body through the Streets of the City, in a Sort of Triumph, almoſt naked, being only laid on a Board, cover'd with ſome Straw, and carried on four Men's Shoulders, and buried it in the ſame Grave, having firſt fill'd the Coffin with ſlack'd Lime.

* He confeſs'd to the Hangman, that he was 33 Years of Age.

The following Account Turpin *gave of himſelf, to the Topſman, the Week after his Condemnation, and repeated the ſame Particulars to him again at the Gallows; which being taken down from his own Mouth, are as follows:*

THAT he was bred a Butcher, and ſerv'd five Years of his Time very faithfully in *White-Chappel*; but falling into idle Company, he began to take unlawful Meaſures to ſupport his Extravagance, and went ſome times on the Highway on Foot, and met with ſeveral ſmall Booties; his not being detected therein, gave

him Encouragement to ſteal Horſes, and purſu
his new Trade in *Epping* Foreſt on Horſeback
which he had continued about ſix Years.   Having been out one whole Day, without meeting
any Booty, and being very much tired, he laid
himſelf down in the Thicket, and turn'd hi
Horſe looſe, having firſt taken off the Saddle
when he wak'd, he went to ſearch after hi
Horſe, and meeting with Mr. *Thompſon*'s Servant
he enquir'd, if he had ſeen his Horſe ? To whicl
Thompſon's Man anſwer'd, *That he knew nothing
of* Turpin's *Horſe, but that he had found* Tur
pin ; and accordingly preſented his Blunderbuſ
at *Turpin*, who inſtantly jumping behind a broad
Oak, avoided the Shot, and immediately fir'd
Carbine at *Thompſon*'s Servant, and ſhot him
dead on the Spot ; one Slug went through hi
Breaſt, another thro' his Right Thigh, and
third thro' his Groin.   This done, he withdrew
to a Yew Tree hard by, where he conceal'
himſelf ſo cloſely, that though the Noiſe
Mr. *Thompſon*'s Man's Blunderbuſs and his ow
Carbine had drawn together a great Number
People about the Body, yet he continued und
cover'd two whole Days and one Night in th
Tree ; when the Company was all diſpers'd,
got out of the Foreſt, and took a Black Hor
out of a Cloſe near the Road, and there bein
People working in the Field at a Diſtance,
threw ſome looſe Money amongſt them, ar
made off ; but afterwards the ſame Evening ſto
a Cheſnut Mare, and turning his Black Hor
looſe, made the beſt of his Way for *London*.

Some Time after he returned to the Foreſt again, and attempted to rob Captain *Thompſon* and his Lady in an open Chaiſe, but the Captain firing a Carbine at him, which miſs'd, *Turpin* fir'd a Piſtol after the Captain, which went through the Chaiſe between him and his Lady, without any further Damage, than tearing the left Sleeve of his Coat; the Captain driving hard, and being juſt in Sight of a Town, *Turpin* thought it not proper to purſue him any farther.

Next he ſtop'd a Country Gentleman, who clapping Spurs to his Horſe, *Turpin* followed him, and firing a Piſtol after him, which lodg'd two Balls in his Horſe's Buttocks, the Gentleman was oblig'd to ſurrender: He robb'd him of Fifty Shillings; and asking him if that was all, and the Gentleman ſaying he had no more, *Turpin* ſtrip'd him, and found two Guineas more in his Pocket Book, out of which he return'd him Five Shillings, but at the ſame Time told the Gentleman, it was more than he deſerved, becauſe of his Intention to have cheated him.

After this he ſtop'd a Farmer in *Epping* Foreſt, who had been to *London* to ſell Hay, and took from him Fifty Shillings; and hearing of ſeveral Coaches coming that Way, laid wait for them; but they being inform'd of the frequent Robberies in thoſe Parts, took another Road.

Another Time meeting a Gentleman and a Lady on Horſeback, in a Lane near the Foreſt, he ſtop'd them, and preſented a Piſtol, at which the Lady fell into a Swoon; he took from the Gentleman ſeven Guineas and ſome Silver, and from the Lady a Watch, a Diamond Ring, one Guinea, and fifteen Shillings in Silver.

He likewife own'd, that he was a Confederate with one *King*, who was executed in *London* fome Time fince; and that, once being very near taken, he fir'd a Piftol among the Crowd, and by Miftake fhot the faid *King* into the Thigh, who was coming to refcue him.

He alfo confefs'd the Facts of which he was convicted; but faid, many Things had been laid to his Charge, of which he was innocent. Tho' 'tis very probable he was guilty of feveral Robberies not here mention'd, yet this was the whole Confeffion that the Topfman could get from him.

F I N I S.